TRY GOD

LEAH HERNANDEZ

Purposeful Millennials Publishing

Contents

Ordering Information:

Quantity sales. Special discounts are available on quantity purchases by corporations, associations, and others. Orders by U.S. trade bookstores and wholesalers. Please contact:
leah@purposefulmillennialspublishing.com

Printed in the United States of America

This book is dedicated to the next generation who are constantly fighting to live righteous in such an unrighteous world. To my family I love each and every one of you. This book marks the shift in our family.

Do not consider this as simply a book; consider it as an interactive experience. Throughout these upcoming pages, I will be using myself as an example of someone who was "raised in the church," someone who went through the motions of "playing church," someone who lived a life that contradicted her faith. I am an example of someone who drifted so far away from God that by the time I began receiving my tests of faith, I was already knocked down by the cares of the world, by temptations and by tribulations that God tried to tell me would come.

I am someone who knows firsthand how intimidating it can be to drift away from God after indulging in so much sin. Don't let my appearance fool you; I was far from perfect, even after being in the church and putting up the façade of being saved.

I was someone who could recite Bible verse after verse, be attentive in every service and actively participate in the call and response of sermons and still find the desire to be active in the world. There lay the problem, I was in the church my entire life, but the church was not in me.

After so many failed tests, after beating myself up time and time again for returning to habits I swore I had put down, after going through the motions Sunday after Sunday, I came to the realization that it was time to stop playing church.

When I say it's time to stop playing church I'm referring to the façade, the fake, the phony and the double life we find ourselves living as "so-called" believers. I'm referring to the complacency that we have in our relationship with God; our following the same routine of going to church, praying using repetitions, and *acting* like Christians. This is the same routine that we have been following all our lives that ultimately leads us nowhere.

Somewhere in our journey in Christ we, somehow, picked up the habit of "going through the motions". You know, doing the things that Christians "ought to do" rather than committing ourselves to spiritual growth. As believers, we have become committed walking in what I call a "motionless walk" in our spiritual lives, and this motionless walk is leading us to death.

We have become the devil's playground for dead Christians. Dead Christians are those who live the life that a Christian is supposed to live but do not save souls and is not fruitful. Dead Christians are believers who know of God, have had an encounter with Him, but in some part of their spiritual journey have rejected the life that God has called them to live. Dead Christians have committed to a stagnant relationship with God and as a result, have strayed away from the spiritual course that they once walked with diligence and a fervent spirit.

In this book, my prayer is that I am able to encourage those who drifted away from God somewhere in their spiritual journey. I pray that I can encourage you to find the focus, discipline and motivation to fully commit to God, breaking the cycle of comfortability and seeking growth.

Finally, with the many lessons that I attempt to provide in the following pages of this book, I offer the most important prayer that we can have in our spiritual walk: I pray that we never stop pursuing God and that we always desire more of Him.

Understanding the Cycle

IN ORDER TO find a solution to a problem, the problem must first be identified. Identifying a problem is done in two parts: defining the problem and determining how you got to the problem in the first place.

The problem at hand: complacency.

As Christians, we oftentimes find ourselves practicing complacency in our relationship with God. The problem with complacency in our spiritual lives, however, soon turns into problems with complacency in our everyday lives. We recognize complacency in our spiritual lives when we begin to lose that desire to pursue God; we notice that fire that we once had to walk in the way of God burning out. Oftentimes, we do not realize that as our fire for God begins to burn out, every aspect of our life will, ultimately, follow suit.

As soon as you become comfortable in your motionless walk with God, you begin to compromise all aspects of your life: your family, your career, your health, your aspirations, goals, morals and the list goes on. Though your life may not be noticeably poor, you may drive a decent car, work a well-paying job, and have a stable family, you, somehow, still feel a void in your life, a void that cannot be filled with material possessions or man's affections. You are grateful for your job, your family and your material blessings, but every night when you lay down *something* inside of you still feels empty and you can't quite put your finger on what *it* is. Well, I will let you in on a secret: that void and emptiness is the lack of God's presence in your life.

As believers, we often drift away from God, rededicate our lives to Him making the decision to remain faithful, then, somewhere along the way, we find ourselves getting comfortable with where we are in our relationship with Him. This comfortability quickly becomes stagnation.

When Complacency Leads to Stagnation

Stagnation is defined as being still, not moving, not progressing and lacking activity.

As we become stagnant in our relationships with God, we notice that the stagnation in our spiritual lives trickles down into our personal, professional, social and every other part of our lives. We notice this because when we are on good terms in our spiritual walk, we often withstand test and trials more easily, we are less confused about God's plan, and we are more receptive to God's voice. As our fire begins to die down and we move into a stagnant place, our lives seem to take a turn. Oftentimes, when we face adversity, we find ourselves in a state of confusion, feeling so distant from God that we do not have the spiritual strength to withstand and understand trials and tribulations. We, once again, find ourselves back on our knees at the foot of the altar, crying out to God. We begin to question: "How did I get here again? Why do I keep drifting further and further away from God? Why is it so hard for me to submit to God completely and give Him my life?"

At this moment, we resubmit our lives and start our spiritual walk anew, but as time progresses, we slip back into our old ways, going through the motions: praying half-heartedly, going to church out of routine but not taking the message and applying it to our lives and treating God like a lifetime subscription—pay once and done.

This is what we know as "the cycle." Christians who know of God, are familiar with the word, but have never had a committed authentic relationship with God and never experienced a personal interaction with Jesus Christ are subject to, and oftentimes, get sucked into The Cycle.

For example, I was one of the many who grew up in church. I knew the difference between right and wrong, but somehow, I caught myself being anywhere and every-where including in and out of God's presence…

Follow God's example, therefore, as dearly loved children and walk in the way of love, just as Christ loved us and gave himself up for us as a fragrant offering and sacrifice to God.

Ephesians 5:1-2

When I was a child my mother made it a priority for her children to attend church. By the time I was a teenager, church had become just another task that I marked off my daily "to-do" list. As I grew older, however, I slowly began to understand why my mother made sure that the family attended church faithfully and attempted to make sure that we knew the meaning of it all.

As a young child, I was introduced to God through all

the cool Bible stories. I knew of how Jonah was swallowed by a whale and how Moses parted the Red Sea. I could recite information from any well-known Bible story, but I could never take the Biblical information presented in the stories and apply it to my own life. At the time, all the Bible was to me was a series of stories; it was never received as an instructions manual. Church taught me the Bible, praise and worship, the Ten Commandments and the difference between right and wrong; one thing that the church didn't teach was the means of obtaining a real relationship with God. Therefore, as a teenager, I never learned.

By the time I reached the sixth grade I was deeply involved in the church. I was on the praise dance team and I was heavily involved with the youth ministry. Volunteering my time for the church was never a question or a fight with me because the older I got, the more I began to find a deeper love for the church.

Though I was deep in the church, I still had not truly experienced Jesus Christ, nor did I have a personal relationship with Him at this point in my life. I was so involved with the church simply out of my love for volunteering and for the feeling I got for "doing good deeds," but the more I gave myself to the church as a volunteer, the more I began to believe that my good deeds were a means to salvation. The more and more I served at the church the more and more I thought my place in heaven was reserved.

Watching others is just an example of an authentic relationship with God, but we can't rely on that to fuel our own relationship.

As a child I didn't understand the concept of having a relationship with God. I knew that I needed a relationship with Him, but I did not know how to obtain it. The idea of loving a God that I could not even see, hear, or feel was a bit challenging. So, instead of truly trying to understand the idea of building a relationship with something I did not know was truly there, I substituted the relationship with religion. You know, I did things that Christians were "supposed to do." I read my Bible, volunteered at the church, took notes during service, and raised my hands during praise and worship. The scary thing is, I became really good at it too. I was mastering the routine of religion. After years of practice, I had mastered the art of, ultimately, *playing church*.

Growing up in the church, I watched others who I believed had encountered Christ. I never realized that although I could copy and paste what they did, I did not have an actual relationship with Jesus Christ. I just knew how to make it seem as though I did, as though I had it all together. I knew exactly when to raise my hands a little higher during praise and worship, close my eyes a little harder, and when I was really pretending, even go down on my knees. If someone were to glance over at me, they would think I was really feeling the Holy Spirit, but truthfully, I was really just feeling the beat of the drums and the worship leaders that were singing.

But why did I do that? Why did I feel obligated to put on a façade that I was experiencing something I was not? Maybe I felt like if I didn't "make it look" like I was having a revival and feeling Gods' presence I would be the odd ball out. I mean, seriously, if I wasn't experiencing the presence of God, why was I working so hard to fake it? I reflect now and I think of how in a house full of worshippers, I managed to fake the worship for years, undetected. I wonder if I actually went undetected, if I thought I was fooling others, but in actuality, the only person I was fooling was myself. Most of all, I wonder how many people around me were doing the same thing.

My façade continued throughout high school, and I felt myself drifting further and further away from the Spirit. But instead of correcting the problem, I decided to let it persist; after all, I knew that I could make it appear that my relationship with God was healthy and thriving. This was when I began to truly "go through the motions."

Because I had grown up in the church I knew what I needed to do in order to "look the part" of a Christian. From the outside looking in, no one noticed the private life outside of church that I had been living: the partying, the smoking, the drinking. All of that was my Monday through Saturday activities, but come Sunday, I was up bright and early to go to church.

To be successful in my double life I had to keep the church at an arms' length. I never allowed myself to be too connected with the members of the church. See, I knew that the closer I allowed the church, the higher the risk of blowing my secret. I had friends in the church; we shared great memories and times, but those memories were of times only spent on Sunday between the hours of nine o'clock in the morning to twelve in the afternoon. If people began to see who I truly was outside of the four walls of church, then this whole double life and my chance at having the best of both worlds would not last.

No man can serve two masters: for either he will hate the one, and love the other; or else he will hold to the one, and despise the other. Ye cannot serve God and mammon.

Matthew 6:24

Even with the parties and the double life, I felt torn. I was doing what I wanted to do and living how I wanted to live, but I was not satisfied. Because I knew of the Word of God deep down inside, I *knew* I wasn't saved, and I knew that the secret life I was living prohibited me from gaining that personal relationship with God.

The cycle doesn't end here, at one point in your life you'll experience the "prodigal son" moment. After time goes by, and you realize that the world doesn't have the ability to fulfill all the pipe dreams it promised you, there will come a period when you fall back on the church. You will go to service one day and listen attentively to the sermon, just knowing that Pastor is speaking directly to you and no one else, and as the choir's praises saturate the atmosphere and the Spirit of God begins to move, you will feel a pull on your heart. As altar call opens, thoughts race through your head: "Should I go?" you will ask yourself. "What will the church say about me? My parents hold positions in the church; I'll make them look bad." All of these thoughts will attempt to dissuade you from moving towards the altar. It will become time to make a decision: Will you rededicate your life to God, or will you continue to sit in your pool of unforgiven sin and allow the world to silence your cry out to God?

Finally, you decide to give your life to God… again. Then what happens? You listen to the gospel station on Pandora for the rest of the day, and you wake up Monday morning and immediately gravitate towards the same mindset you had Friday evening.

This marks The Cycle.

The Roadmap to a Relationship

What do we do after deliverance? What are the necessary steps we need to take in order to not fall right back into what we came from? It is time that we stop entertaining the lifestyle of a wishy washy Christian or a convenient Christian. "I'm only going to praise God when He finally gets me what I've been praying for, I'm only going to fully commit to God when I grow up a little more and experience the college experience." Somehow we have left room for a gray area when it comes to being a Christian. Gray area in the way we live our lives, gray area in the amount of energy we give towards God, gray area in the parts of the Bible we chose not to live out because of convenience.

The truth of the matter is this cycle the Christian community continues to fall victim to and this double life we find ourselves living only does an injustice to us. Because if we base our relationship with God off complacency and convenience that becomes the foundation of our faith. And when the big bad wolf comes to knock our house down we will fall, because our house was never made with durable bricks. Instead we made it out of feathers: what we felt like doing, how we felt like praising God, how we felt like living our life, how we felt like using our talents and how we felt like submitting to God. When all along our foundation should have been scripture, prayer, meditation, relationship with God and connection to the Holy Spirit. Again, you are not alone. In fact I was the naïve one who built my foundation exactly off of convenience and stagnation so when my big bad wolf came he knocked my house all the way down.

As you begin to grow in your relationship with God the only way that the relationship will work is if you seek Him with *all* of your heart. Because all of our hearts are different, our relationships with God will not be the same as anyone else's. No matter what others relationships with God look like, you have to create your own. You cannot copy and paste the way your mother praises and lives for God or imitate your favorite YouTube preacher because then the realness of the relationship between you and God is now compromised. When you try to replicate a Godly relationship that you've witnessed, your relationship with God becomes forced and unauthentic. Instead of flowing in your relationship with God, you simply enter into another cycle of doing things by habit and forceful nature.

Oftentimes when taking our spiritual journey, we become frustrated because we attempt to imitate the journeys of others. Treating a spiritual relationship as a roadmap filled with directions, we think that if the endpoint, salvation, is similar between all people, then the journey and the roads that are taken to get there should also be similar. This is the most incorrect thought that we could have.

We witness others' journeys, but many times, we only see their blessings, but we don't see their lessons. You conclude that if you take the same spiritual steps as your best friend who seems to be so wrapped up in the love of God that all she receives is His blessings that you will receive blessings and your life will resemble hers. But, it doesn't.

You get frustrated because you're doing exactly what your friend is doing, but she is being blessed and you're not. The reason why you're not receiving the same results is because you have a different journey. The way each of us experience God is different. We all have our own unique way of communication with God. Some of us may hear from God through signs, symbols and numbers, others may hear from God through mediation and solitude. We all have our own specific needs from God. Some of us may need love and attention while others may need security and protection. The point is everyone's relationship with God is different they're not made to be the same. Once we realize that each of our relationships is different, then and only then can we appreciate our own spiritual journeys.

2

The Spiritual Fire

THAT FIRE you gained from the altar on Sunday afternoon lasted only but 24 hours. But why? Why can't we keep that burning desire in us that we experience Sunday to last throughout the week?

Listed below are simply a few ways in which we allow our fires to die.

1. Lack of Sacrifice

As believers we often find comfort in knowing that we serve such an amazing, wonder-working God that we expect Him to do all the work Himself. We reflect and see how far He brought us and conclude that He has the power to provide the sacrifice that we need to ignite our spiritual fires and keep them burning. We expect God to do all the work for upholding the relationship while we reap all of the benefits, but we must realize that in our spiritual relationships with God, just as in our physical relationships with man, the efforts must be equal on both ends.

There's a popular Christian song called "Fill Me Up,"

and it says, "If you provide the fire, I'll provide the sacrifice. If you pour out your spirit, I will open up inside." See the problem is not that God does not supply us with what we need to keep our fires burning; it's the lack of our sacrifice that blocks our personal relationship with Him. The lack of our sacrifice prevents the grace of God to overflow in our life.

In your relationship with God, you must fully examine what you contribute and make sure that what you give is more than what you expect to receive. You must ask yourself, "What do I have to offer God? How am I benefiting His Kingdom? How am I glorifying His Holy name?" As these questions circulate through your mind, and you search for the answers, you must also examine how you contribute to the dying down of your spiritual fire in terms of your sacrifice.

2. Not Spending Time with God

You cannot expect God to bless your life everyday if the only day you "spend" with Him is Sunday morning.

Think of it this way: When you leave your house what's one thing you make sure you keep with you? A phone charger? If your days are anything like mine; my phone is not going to last me the whole day if I do not charge it at some point in my day. I am constantly making calls, sending emails, shooting texts and not to mention all the battery I use being on all of my apps. There is no way I am going to keep my phone fully charged all day without plugging it in at some point.

Think of your spirit as a battery and the Word as a charger. You cannot depend solely on Sunday afternoon service to keep your spiritual battery fully charged throughout the entire week. You must consistently charge your spirit as you go through life. Whether you start your morning off with a prayer, or you go to a Bible study during the week, you must continue to fill your spirit with spiritual energy.

The church house should not be the only time you spend time with God. As the Bible tells us, we, a community of believers, are the church. 1 Corinthians explains the structure of the church, and how we as Christians make up the fullness of the church. The Word reads, "Now you are the body of Christ, and each one of you is a part of it. And God has placed in the church first of all apostles, second prophets, third teachers, then miracles, then gifts of healing, of helping, of guidance, and of different tongues" (1 Corinthians 12: 27-28).

The scripture provides a perfect example of how the works of the church should not be confined to the building rather, we must use the spiritual gifts and knowledge that we have regarding the church in our everyday lives. Using God's gifts constantly lives as testaments of the church and as examples of God's glory.

Every day that we live, we must walk as examples of God. We must fill ourselves with His presence, meditate on His Word, listen closely to His voice and take all that we get from Him and return it to the world, offering the gift of ministry and sharing the gospel, not only in our words but more so in our deeds.

The church building is simply a place to fellowship and to receive some instruction regarding God. The church should not be the one and only source to receive God. We must find multiple sources to receive God that way we will never run dry of Him.

3. The Idea of Coming to God "Perfect"

But the Pharisees and the teachers of the law who belonged to their sect complained to his disciples, "Why do you eat and drink with tax collectors and sinners?" Jesus answered them, "It is not the healthy who need a doctor, but the sick. I have not come to call the righteous, but sinners to repentance."

Luke 5:30-32

Many think and truly believe that God's love is reserved for those who are perfect. So, in order to gain God's love, many feel the need to change themselves: their personalities, habits, physical, mental and emotional characteristics. Many believe that they have to stop sinning completely, begin reading the Bible every day, and go to church three times a week before they can come to God. Does God want you to read your Bible more? Yes! Would He love to see your face at church more often? Of course! But, does He expect you to change your entire life over night? Definitely not!

God knows that none of us are capable of being perfect. God wants us to come to Him regardless of how broken and messed up we are. He doesn't want someone who feels like they have it all together and needs no guidance; He can't work with that. God can heal and fix the broken and messed up people, molding them into what He wants them to be, but He can't work on the person that is already "perfect."

Sometimes we look at others and they seem to have everything figured out, spiritually, professionally, personally and we begin to believe that we have to be the same way to come to God and experience the loving relationship that they seem to have with Him. We fail to realize that there's no such thing as coming to God perfect. Oftentimes, the thought that we must be whole before we can come to God is the enemy planting into our minds a seed of fear and inadequacy. We feel as though we are not worthy to come to God for help, fearing what His response to us may be after so many years of running from Him, rejecting Him and choosing the way of the world over His way, but in all actuality, God just wants us to come. Just as we are.

The pressure of being perfect is too much for any man to bear. The enemy has used that as a tactic to drive fear into us to make us believe that no matter how hard we try, we will never be good enough for God. When in fact, God is not expecting perfection; He's expecting humility, just a pure heart that wants to know Him better. We work so hard trying to change ourselves that we do not realize that we are taking on God's job. At no time does any scripture imply that we must change ourselves, rather, we should allow God to change us.

Out of fear, you begin to play the waiting game with God. You think, "I'll get closer to God when my life is together, when I graduate college, get a family, settle down, catch up on my bills, stop sinning" and get it together in every other part of life that requires you taking responsibility. This is not always the best idea. You miss out on a relationship with God trying to become what you think God expects you to be rather than simply being who you are—human. If you wait to get your life together to build a relationship with God, you will never have a relationship with Him because, despite popular belief, you can't get your life together on your own, and God knows this, which is why He is always ready to step in to help once you ask for guidance, and oftentimes, even before then.

The problem is too many of us try doing it on our own until we wake up three years later and realize our relationship with God didn't get any better; we just got better at faking like it did. Getting to know God is an interactive effort, so stop blocking God out and allow Him to do a work in your life. There is no room for pride, fear, or insecurity when trying to build a relationship with God. Simply ask Him for help, and open your heart to let Him in so that He can heal you and make you whole.

4. Occupying Your Time with the Wrong Things

What we allow to occupy our time can also be causing the death of our fires. Bad habits, toxic relationships, sex, drugs, and alcohol abuse are only a few of the many things we do daily that dim our fire for God. We spend so much time tending to things that do nothing for our spiritual fires that we do not realize that it is dying us out.

I can ensure you that the more you continue to fill yourself up with God on a consistent basis, unnecessary thoughts that consume much of your time and energy, the same time and energy you could be using to think on things that are good, and honest, and righteous, will begin to fade away.

5. Running Away from Your Purpose

The dilemma many of us have is that we do not know our purpose. In order to find your purpose, you must find who you are, and finding who you are comes with knowing who God is and building a relationship with Him. You may block your purpose because you are truly fearful. Oftentimes, we are fearful because we understand that knowing our purpose in God will probably reveal to us the goals and desires that we have for ourselves are not in the plans that God has for us.

We must seek God's heart and pray that each and every one of our desires align with God's desires for us.

Rejecting the idea of vain glory and selfish ambition, we must dismantle the idea that our life is our own. It is nearly impossible to live for God and devote your life to Him if you do not know your purpose in God.

Tending to Your Fire

Jesus replied: "Love the Lord your God with all your heart and with all your soul and with all your mind."

Matthew 22:37

Oftentimes, I found myself on fire for God. I would get these sudden sparks of energy that made me want to live for God, to put all my efforts into growing in my relationship with God. I would start a new Bible reading plan, set a new prayer schedule, and buy journals and devotionals to help me with my new spiritual journey. I would literally be on fire for God—reading my Bible for hours a day, praying and communicating with God more heavily than ever, watching sermons and consciously looking for ways to incorporate everything that I had been learning in my spiritual life. This would go on for some time, but after a while, I would begin to lose that motivation to seek God. I would begin to cut my Bible readings down, my prayers would become shorter and less heart filled, and I would not think about Biblical principles as much in my everyday life. This was my fire dying out.

I knew what caused my fire to die, I could even sense it dying out, but how could I tend to my fire to keep it burning?

One way I've learned to tend to my fire is by eliminating distractions.

Many times we are not able to tend to our fires because we are so busy tending to others. We are taking sticks from God's fire and putting them into our relationship fires, our financial fires, our personal fires, and any other fire that consumes us daily. We do this not realizing that if only we put all of our sticks into one fire, the fire that has the most potential to grow, then that fire will grow so great, and it will, inevitably, consume everything around it. If we used all of our time, energy, and resources to tend to our spiritual fires, then every other aspect of our lives would be consumed by our spiritual fire.

Your spiritual fire has the power to clean and renew all areas of your life, but it cannot do that if it is not tended to. You have to release yourself of all distractions that are consuming you so that your focus and energy can go into growing and maintaining your spiritual fire.

Appreciating Isolation

Our relationship fires are, oftentimes, the fires that we tend to most. In an effort to keep our loved ones happy, to nurture growing relationships and repair broken ones, we often put so much time and energy into adding sticks and stirring up the charred remains of our relationship fires that we neglect our spiritual fires.

And this is exactly what the devil wants us to do.

In order to upkeep your spiritual fire so that you will know how to tend to your relationship fire, believe it or not, you must practice isolation. In practicing isolation, you must be able to discern between spirits. Sometimes it seems as though when you begin to isolate yourself to be alone with God, the devil uses such times as a challenge to get closer to you, fearful that the wall that you are beginning to build to keep the world out may actually work. In these times, however, you must be mindful of the devil's ploys.

Rather than sending an enemy or a stranger into your life to disrupt your isolation, the devil will send someone that is already close to you. The devil will not send someone who can be easily identified as an enemy, rather someone who you will never suspect.

So, be cautious of the spirits that are coming in and out of your life during your time of spiritual growth. Constantly pray that God will give you the power to discern between them so that you can properly protect your spirit and guard your heart.

3

Breaking the Cycle: Trusting in Man vs. Trusting in God

Stop trusting in mere humans, who have but a breath in their nostrils. Why hold them in esteem.

Isaiah 2:22

TRUST IS the willingness and comfortability of fully believing in someone, which often presents a dilemma. In our relationships and interactions with man, we oftentimes put our trust in them believing that they have our best interest at heart, or that we are a priority in their lives. So, in our relationships, we oftentimes put the trust that we should put in God in man.

We trust our friends to give us sound advice but never go to God to hear His answers to our questions. We trust our parents and significant others to protect us, provide for us, and love us unconditionally but never truly think on how God already offers protection, provision and unconditional love. We trust man to have our best interest at heart when making decisions that affect us but we never ask God of His intentions for us, the same God who had our will planned before we were even conceived in our mothers' wombs.

We do not realize it, but we put so much trust in man that when God asks us to trust Him, we think we have no more trust to give.

We put so much trust in man, who God had already told us would err, that when one bad occurrence happens, all of our trust is shattered, our feelings are hurt, and we are thrown into a state of emotional chaos not understanding how someone we trusted so much could betray us. So, as a result of this broken trust, we begin to have trust issues, and many times, those trust issues with physical relationships are carried into our spiritual relationships. Furthermore, we brought our trust issues this world caused into our relationship with God—our biggest mistake.

There is no way we can obtain a real authentic relationship with God with trust issues. It just simply will not work. A part of our foundation with God is based solely on trust. Trust is believing that God is everything He promises to be and that He will do everything He promises He will do. God promises that He will never leave us nor forsake us, that He is the way the truth and the light and that He will give everlasting life to anyone who believes in Him. God makes many grand promises, and trust is simply believing in our hearts that each and every one of God's promises holds true.

Now the question is: how do I trust God when everything or everyone I trusted let me down?

First separate the two (God and man). No longer can you put God and your ex, or God and your former friend or even God and your mother on the same pedestal. God is in an entirely different realm than one of your close comrades who broke your trust because He is supernaturally more loving, more caring, and more dependable than the one who betrayed you.

In order to put your trust, the same trust you thought was broken forever, into the hands of God you simply have to try God.

My grandma had a necklace that said Try God, and when I asked her what that meant she said "Just as it says, try God!" Just like you try a new dish for the first time or try a new hobby or activity you, literally, just have to do it. The key is when you try God; you must go back to the definition of trust which is to willingly believe. I guarantee you that the moment you truly, and I mean truly, try God, He will reveal himself to you in ways you could not even imagine.

The Faith Crisis

The faith of the people closest to you will affect your view on faith. Meaning if you're constantly surrounded by people who have little to no faith and think the worst of every situation, their spirit is going to rub off on yours. You must protect your spirit. If you do not do all that is in your power to protect your spirit, you may end up in a faith crisis.

A faith crisis is the disbelief that God has power over any and all situations. Heck! A faith crisis is simply the lack of believing period.

Some symptoms of a faith crisis are hesitation in submission to God, disbelief in the promises of God, and lastly not living the lifestyle as a child of God.

The identity crisis we found ourselves in simply played as the gateway to the faith crisis we found ourselves in later down the line. When someone is unsure in their faith, they often have nothing to lean on, hope for and depend on.

The devil attacks our faith because he knows the power of faith and where faith can take us.

John 15:7: "If you remain in me and my words remain in you, ask whatever you wish, and it will be done for you."

It is because of the truth and the power in scriptures such as the one listed above that illustrate to us what faith can do. As long as I stay connected to God and His word remains in me, then whatever I ask for, I will receive, and the same applies to you!

No wonder the devil attacks our belief in God, because of promises such as these. If the devil is able to deflect faith in God then, he can successfully block all promises from God. Could you imagine how much more successful people would be if they had faith? With faith, we can break the cycle of poverty, generational curses, mental diseases any stronghold or spirit of bondage that is attacking our lives!

In order to escape a faith crisis, we have to change our mindsets. Think about the law of attraction. If you constantly think on good things, good things will come to you. Likewise, if you constantly have negative thoughts, negative happenings will occur. The Word tells us that whatsoever things are pure, honest and of good report, we should think on those things (Philippians 4:8).

Our mindset is the biggest determiner of our faith so if we can shift our mindset to think that all things will work together, just as God promises, those positive thoughts will trickle down into our spiritual lives. This marks the beginning of having faith.

How to Play the Cards You Are Dealt

Growing up, my family was really big on playing games during family functions, especially card games. A very common game that we would play was "Gin Rummy." In this game, like many other card games you are dealt a hand, and it is up to you to make the best out of the hand you are dealt in order to win the game. At some point in the game, almost everyone is dealt a bad hand. My grandmother always had a way of flipping her bad hand into a win; she hardly ever lost a game of "Gin Rummy."

After an uncountable amount of losses, I got tired of losing so, I put my pride aside and asked her, "Grandma what's your secret? How do you always win?"

Her answer: "I never show through my facial expressions I was dealt a bad hand and I don't make reckless moves that would lead my opponent into thinking I was dealt a poor hand."

In the game of life, I believe that we are all dealt a bad hand at one point, but the choice of how we play that hand is ultimately up to us.

Have you ever heard that saying, "life is 10% what happens to you and 90% how you react to it?" Well, as cliché as it sounds, it is extremely true. In life, you will have some hardships, but how you react to the hardships will determine your situation.

Much like my grandma's poker face in "Gin Rummy," we cannot show the enemy any fear. No matter how bad my grandmother's hand was, she kept her composure throughout the game, and she didn't give her opponents an open door to take advantage of her because of the cards she was dealt. The same concept applies to or lives. If we make reckless decisions based on our circumstances, we will have no control over our situations and we will begin to lose power over our own lives. In all situations, no matter how chaotic or how far we went left from the designated plan, we must keep our composure and not allow the enemy to see us fearful.

Some of the best card players have the ability to win games despite the bad hands they are given because they believe more in their own ability than they believe in their opponents' strength. They have enough faith in themselves that no matter what they are dealt, they know that the cards are still in their possession so they have the authority to flip the game around to go in their favor.

Even if you are currently living through your trial, you have the power and control over your life, no one else. What you choose to do with the hand you are dealt is ultimately up to you.

The Bible tells us that the enemy is like a roaring lion just waiting to devour. You cannot allow your challenges to loosen the grip that you have over your life because as soon as the enemy can sense that you are beginning to lose faith and hope that is when he strikes.

The truth of the matter is bad things happen to everyone. Tests and trials are inevitable, and we will all come across obstacles in our lives. We seem to think that if we trust and believe in God, we are exempt from struggles. Wrong! God does not magically make all of our problems disappear; rather He faces our problems with us so that we never face them alone.

We must realize that, despite our situations, we must believe and have faith in God that He will not lead us into a path of destruction.

Instead of lashing out and trying to escape the storms of life, we have to find the peace of God in the middle of the water.

When going through a trying time it is vital that we speak life over our situations and remind ourselves that our trials are only temporary. We must constantly remind ourselves that if we keep believing, not only will we gain so much more strength, but we will gain a tremendous amount of faith.

The Three P's: Perspective, Priorities, and Position

Our perspective, priorities and position all play a vital role in our lives. If the three do not align with one another, it is almost impossible to reach your moment of achievement. Your moment of achievement can be anything: a promotion at work, marriage, graduating college, mending your family together, *anything*.

During the time when I would imitate others relationship with God as a result I received nothing, and because of that I wanted my moment of achievement to be a relationship with God. In order to obtain that, my perspective, priorities and position all had to be on one accord and truthfully at that point in my life, they were not. My perspective led me to want a relationship with God, but I was not placing myself in a position to acquire one, nor was I setting such desire as the top priority. My position was all out of wack for many different reasons: my pride, my lack of self-will, my inability to face the demons that I was battling with and my actions behind closed doors. On top of that, my priorities were completely out of order. I placed almost everything in my life above God, school, work, relationships, hobbies and the list goes on. See the thing that I did not fully grasp was that once I placed God at the center of my life, everything else would have no choice but to align perfectly.

The case may be the same or very similar for you. You could have the right perspective and want to make changes in your life to reach your moment of achievement, but you find yourself being in positions that deter you from pressing toward your mark. Or, you may be in the right position but your priorities are out of order. Whatever the case may be, your perspective, or your thought process and interpretations of certain situations must be on one accord with your position. Your position is the spiritual, mental, emotional, and even a physical place that you are in. A good position is not just the church, but it is any place that allows you the space to grow and develop in your faith and in your relationship with God. For example, you can't put yourself in a position to fall into temptation like in the bed with an unbeliever that you know is not good for your spirit, a party full of smoking and drinking or any other place that the devil resides, and expect your perspective to change and your priorities to be ordered.

You must be open to being placed in positions, to set priorities, and to redefine your perspective that will allow you spiritual growth and development.

Acknowledging the Holy Spirit

Why should we acknowledge the Holy Spirit? Who is the Holy Spirit? How is acknowledging the Holy Spirit going to help me break the cycle of complacency in my relationship with God?

The Holy Spirit is a messenger between us and God. The Holy Spirit guides our steps, leads us in the right directions and directs us on God's path.

Have you ever been in a situation where something inside of you told you not to go somewhere, turn down an offer, or even simply go right instead of left? You may consider this a gut feeling, so you listen. Maybe you forget about that gut feeling you had, but soon the decision you made represents itself in the outcome that it had. You look back and realize that there was a good reason why you had that thought, maybe you were saved from impending danger or maybe you avoided some sort of loss. Those thoughts that you had, the one's you believed to be gut feelings, were actually acts of the Holy Spirit.

The Holy Spirit serves to intercede on our behalves to guide us in the right direction when we have no idea what direction that is.

Nothing happens by pure coincidence, but all things happen according to God's will, sometimes good, and sometimes seemingly bad. In all things, however, we must acknowledge the Holy Spirit, thanking Him for His guidance and intercessions.

4

The Fear of Living for God

WHEN IT COMES to the topic of living for God, many people begin to feel uneasy, fearful and even uncomfortable. But why is that? Why does the topic of living for God cause so much anxiety? Why does it seem so hard to live for God?

We live in a society and are raising a generation that lives the Word by pieces. We have become so accustomed to picking and choosing the Biblical principles we feel like we can handle, and we turn a blind eye to the instructions from God that we're not willing heed.

Many are fearful to live for God because they do not have a complete understanding of what living for God looks likes. Oftentimes, we have the wrong perception of God and we get caught up in believing that we have to be religious living strictly by the by the book in order to rightfully live for God. When in actuality, all we need is the relationship. The lack of a relationship with God makes room for false perceptions to arise, and that is what breeds fear. We have adopted a set of step by step instructions on

"How to Live for Christ" but we fail to realize that a relationship with God does not require us to hit every point on a list to have a relationship with God. When experiencing a true and authentic relationship with God, God will transform our lives and our lives will, consequently, be reflective of one that is living for God. We lose ourselves and our spiritual direction when we begin to believe that we are supposed to change ourselves, our actions, our attitudes, and our behaviors. But here's the secret: we are not expected to change ourselves; we are required to allow God to change us.

Much like in physical relationships, in order to have a real relationship with God, you must spend time with Him, get to know Him and communicate with Him. You must pursue God, connect with God one on one, understand His desires, His likes and dislikes and His wants and needs. Sometimes, it is difficult for us to live for God because we do not know Him. It is impossible to live for someone, and even more so, give your life to someone, you do not know.

The more you begin to pursue and get to know God the more you'll learn about yourself. See living for God is unique for each person; the way I live my life is completely different from the way you may chose to live your life. Of course all Christians share the same core values like loving one another but the way I show love is different from the way you may show love. The good thing about this is we don't have to pick and chose what we're allowed and not allowed to do because the closer we get to God the better understanding we will have about ourselves.

The Opinions of Others

But whoever disowns me before others, I will disown before my Father in heaven.

Matthew 10:33

Another dilemma that we face when it comes to living for God is allowing the opinions of others determine our next move. Trust and believe I know firsthand how hard it is to be a Christian in the world we live in, let alone a young Christian. The enemy specifically attacks the youth because he knows we are still trying to grow, find ourselves, and understand who we are and why we've been placed on this earth. His goal is to attack us using social media, reality shows, and people we interact with to tempt us with the things of this world. Naturally, our flesh is going to desire the things that are not good for our spirit, but we have to deny our flesh in order to protect our spirit.

Some fear living the life that God called them to live because they fear the thoughts of others. Your friends or family members may not believe in God, and what will they think if they get word that's what you're all about now? Caring about the opinions of others is something we all claim to not do. "I don't care what other people think about me." "They can think or say what they want." But it's about time we actually start believing this instead of just saying it because the scary truth is: if the opinions of others didn't affect you, you would have given your life to God years ago.

Some may even live for Christ but are fearful of professing their faith aloud.

Many believers struggle with being bold for Christ. We want to reap the benefits of living for God but neglect the piece where we actually have to live for God. Some often wonder why people are still on the street, and people aren't getting saved. The answer to that is in the Christian community, we have too many "Closet Christians." A "Closet Christian" is anyone who does not live boldly for Christ, only sharing the good news of God to their close family and friends. If you notice that you fall into any of those categories then we must now reevaluate some things. The effect of being a closet Christian is that people never see God through you. The only way people can see God is if you allow God to use you as a willing vessel. It's time to come out the closet and live boldly for Christ.

Experiencing God's Miracles

Many of us have fallen victim to having fake faith. Fake faith is exactly what it sounds like: pretending to have faith, but in the case where faith is really needed, it is nowhere to be found.

The Word says, "Now faith is confidence in what we hope for and assurance about what we do not see" (Hebrews 11:1).

The scripture above indicates that faith is nothing if you do not have confidence in what you're expecting God to do for you. Faith is not supposed to be logical. But many times, though the Word tells us and shows us time and time again, we look for the reasoning and logic in faith.

The reason why what you're praying for is not happening is because you're continuing to doubt what you're asking for. We claim that we have faith, but we continue to pray for plan A all the while constructing Plan B. If you have faith in Plan A and that God will bring Plan A to completion, why would you even need a Plan B?

If faith exists then doubt could not exist. Likewise, if

doubt exists, then faith could not possibly exist. As Christians, we must know how to operate in our faith.

Along with faith, we must have a spirit of sacrifice, knowing that God can only add to our lives if we subtract from our lives. God can only work His miracles if we allow Him room to do it.

5

Living with Spiritual Baggage

IN THE BOOK OF LUKE, the thirteenth chapter, there is a story told about a woman healed on the Sabbath day. Although this woman has a spirit of infirmity that she had been battling for eighteen years she remained active in the church. After eighteen painful years, this woman was healed after having one interaction with Jesus Christ.

Biblically a spirit of infirmity is defined as a sickness or disease which brings about a phase of discomfort. The Word explains that this disease caused the woman to lie in a bent over position. As I read this story, I began to realize that I and the ailed woman had a few things in common. Just like the woman, I had been living in discomfort and had allowed my infirmities to weigh down on me which caused me to be bent over for eighteen years.

Shortly after analyzing her situation, I realized that I, too, had been carrying a spirit of infirmity. However, like the woman, despite the fact that I carried this weight on me I was still active in the church. Unlike the woman, my spirit of infirmity was not noticeable to others or even myself. I was always lively and happy throughout my childhood so my spirit of infirmity was hard to detect, but it was not until I had an encounter with Christ that I realized what I had been missing. When I began to analyze my situation, I began to question my life. "How could I not have had an encounter with Jesus Christ if I faithfully attended church? I mean, wasn't that the sole purpose of church: to experience God?" I soon came to understand that attending church did not automatically guarantee a personal encounter with Christ. Just like me and this woman, you, too, can be "in the church" and never have had an interaction with Jesus.

I was born into my spirit of infirmity. Just like many young adults, my mother had me at the age of eighteen. Since I was born, the odds were already against me. Once family members and friends discovered the news that my mother was pregnant with me, people began to talk. People gossiped and spoke negatively on her pregnancy. Many people doubted that greatness or success could come from a baby born out of wedlock. Despite all the negative opinions and predictions on my life, my mother did a phenomenal job as a mother.

Now my father was a bit of a rolling stone, he had another daughter prior to me and three after me. After my father found out that he had a fourth child on the way he told my mom that he was going to remove himself from a lifestyle full of gang violence. Many people stated that he actually began to make drastic changes in his life. Unfortunately, that was only a short-lived glory because on April 24, 2000, my father was shot and killed on his way home from visiting his newborn son. I was only three years old so I have no memory of him.

After the death of my father my mother tried to keep in touch with my older half-sister but that did not last because her mother decided to move to a different state. I have never had any encounters with my other half siblings, which growing up I struggled with. What I struggled with the most was my father's side of the family. When my father was alive my mother told me that I would go and visit them when my father would come pick me up which would be maybe once every two weeks. You would think that after the death of my father my "family" would want to continue to stay prevalent in my life, but unfortunately that was not the case. When my father died his parents and the rest of the family rejected and denied me. I thank God for my moms' side of the family because without them I would have never been able to experience what a family truly is.

Thinking that I was adapting to my situations, I was actually just bottling all of my hurt and my pain and letting them build up in my spirit. This was the beginning of my infirmities.

It took years for me to recognize my infirmity, but through self-reflection and growing in faith, I was able to, not only, identify my infirmity, I was able to open up my heart to allow God to heal me of it. You can do the same. What is your infirmity?

When we analyze Luke 13 we see that this woman had been carrying her spirit of infirmity for eighteen years. This is our first clue into finding our spirit of infirmity. Usually our infirmity is something that we have been carrying around for quite some time. This infirmity can be anything from insecurity, an unforgiving heart because of occurrences that happened in the past, a feeling of rejection, a fear of failure, and the list goes on.

Think of a time you felt worthless, inadequate or

depressed. A time you felt like you could never be good enough or could never overcome a tragedy that you had experienced. Think of a time in which you feel your self-worth was compromised. If you can identify a situation in which you experienced any of these feelings, then you have identified the source of your infirmity. Think of your infirmity as a weight. Imagine carrying fifty pounds of bricks on your back. Envision carrying around these bricks for hours that turn into days which turn into weeks. The weeks turn into months, and before you know, years. You spend years in a bent over position, years of discomfort, never experiencing the feeling of standing up tall. Years of indescribable pain. Sounds unbearable right?

See, our infirmities have a way of making us feel weak. They make us feel as though we have no control over our circumstances, when, in fact, we do have control. YOU have control. Oftentimes, in the midst of our pain, in the midst of our internal struggles, we feel so helpless and alone because no friend, sister, no mother or father can help us battle our internal demons. Of course God does give us wise counsel and confidants to help us through our trying times, but our internal battles are ones that we must bear, no one else. This does not mean that we must bear them alone. This means that the only one that can help us bear our infirmities is God.

When your mind tells you that you are unworthy of forgiveness, do not believe it. When your thoughts tell you that your past has the power to determine your future, do not believe it. When your heart tells you that you have wounds too deep to heal, do not believe it. See, no one tells you that you have the power and the will to control your situation, but I'm here to tell you…YOU DO!

You're probably thinking to yourself, "How was this woman was able to get up every day and continue to move forward?" What if I told you that, this woman's circumstances were not too far off from mine and yours? This is actually a reality for majority of us. Just like this woman, we have allowed our infirmities to *alter our position*. Instead of standing up tall in our faith and our purpose we have become accustomed to having a mediocre faith in God and drowning ourselves in the cares of the world. There was a time when I had grown comfortable in my misery and depression that my internal circumstances began to transform my mindset. I began to think that I was going to be in the situation I was in for rest of my life. I thought I would never break the generational curses on my family. I thought that my life was so messed up that not even God would want me.

See my position did not change immediately after my tragedies, my position changed as soon as my mindset changed. My position did not change because of what happened but because of my thoughts toward what happened.

Carrying these infirmities do not only to cause you to live in a state of discomfort but if you carry these infirmities long enough they will cause some *growth defects*. This is what I unfortunately had to learn the hard way. I carried my infirmities for so long that I began to experience growth defects. Physical growth defects are limitations that stop the human body from growing into its full potential. Spiritual infirmities and the growth defects that they create have the same power. Spiritual growth defects stunt the growth of the spirit.

The sooner you identify your infirmities, the quicker you can ask God for healing from them.

The world we live in programs us to hold everything in, including our infirmities. So fearful of being vulnerable, we allow negativity, tragedy and depression to reside in us and then wonder why we are stuck in negative situations, face tragic oppositions, and experience depressed moods, over and over again. Holding in infirmities don't make them go away; they create voids in our spirits, voids that house infirmities that we already have and invite more to come.

Some of you hold infirmities that your family and friends don't even know about; you may think because you're smiling on the outside and moving forward with your life that what happened to you as a child doesn't affect you anymore, but it does. Holding on to all the weight from your past will prevent you from reaching higher levels in your life.

Think of your spiritual journey as a flight and your infirmities as your luggage. Airlines work hard to get travelers to follow the weight requirements for all bags because they know the repercussions of exceeding weight requirements. If there is too much weight on the plane, the plane will not be able to reach higher elevations, and ultimately, its destination.

Just like with a plane, we cannot weigh our lives down with infirmities then expect God to take us to new levels and higher elevations.

6

Confirming Your Calling

"For I know the plans I have for you," declares the Lord, "plans to prosper you and not to harm you, plans to give you hope and a future."

Jeremiah 29:11

NOW THAT WE'VE recognized that knowing and living in our purpose helps break the cycle of spiritual complacency, it's time to identify your purpose and your calling. The truth of the matter is everyone has a ministry; you, yourself, are a walking-breathing-living ministry. Every one of your actions, words, and deeds represent your ministry. As Christians and believers, we are all qualified and, in fact, expected to share the Gospel of Christ. You don't have to stand in front of a pulpit to tell people of the goodness of God. To be truthful, at one point, I actually thought, "What business do I have spreading the gospel? I'm not a preacher or bishop or even head of the church." I used to think it wasn't my place to tell people about Jesus. However, God has called us all to be participators not spec-

40

tators in this spiritual warfare that we, and many others, are fighting. I later learned that if I wanted to live according to my purpose and receive my calling from God, my adherence to God's will was vital.

Many people pass judgment and give critiques about the church but what many fail to realize is that the church is not just a building in which believers fellowship, but the believers themselves are the church. As believers, we are all responsible for driving people closer to God so, if the church is failing then we are all failing. We cannot only expect the preachers, bishops, and gospel artists to bring people to church; we must hold one another accountable for not being active participants in the ministry and the mission. We must realize that though each of us have different gifts and talents, each gift is an equal contribution to the ministry, and therefore, we all carry the same amount of responsibility in the ministry.

In order to find our purpose we must know the difference between what we *can* do and what we are *called* to do. For example, I sing in the shower but this does not mean I am called to be a worship leader. The problem that we are facing as believers is many of us are so afraid to step into our calling that we are stepping into purposes that we were never called to, replacing faith with fear, and consequently, purpose with practice. This world has a way of misguiding us into hobbies and habits that utterly conflict and oppose the purpose that God has over our lives. I wouldn't want to be a janitor my whole life when I was actually predestined to be a CEO.

You're going to hear me say this plenty of times but listen carefully: God has a purpose for everyone. You may feel like this doesn't apply to you because the amount of sin you have surpasses your good works. Whatever your reasoning is, I'm here to tell you that it doesn't matter. No matter the wrong that has been done to you, the wrong that you have done to others, or the mistakes you have made, God does not see you for your shortcomings. He sees you as His child, one who is fearfully and wonderfully made with a unique purpose.

Finding your purpose is not simply for your own benefit, but for others because your purpose will lead you to your ministry.

How Do I Confirm My Calling?

You may ask yourself: "How do I know what I was placed on this earth to do? How am I supposed to find out what my purpose is at such a young age?" Confirming your calling may seem like a daunting task, but it is a simple prayer. That's it! I know you were expecting some unheard of formula that would give you step by step instructions on how to hear the calling over your life, but, and I urge you, don't underestimate the power of prayer. Prayer changes circumstances, reveals God's plan and most importantly, grants you the opportunity to communicate with God. I encourage you to be open to prayer, not be intimidated by it.

At one point in time, I felt that God didn't hear my prayers because of my lifestyle. Sometimes I even felt that my prayers were simply not good enough. Prayer is a direct line of communication between you and God. It is simple conversation. You don't have to change the tone of your voice or use big words in order for God to turn toward your prayer. We don't think twice about conversations we have with our friends, strangers, family members, and even pets so there should be no difference with a conversation with God. Yes, there is a level of respect when praying to God; however, it is nothing to be intimidated by.

A prayer for your calling is as simples as saying, "Dear God I pray for whoever is reading this I pray your will be done in their life; I pray that you reveal to them what their calling and purpose is. Lastly, I pray that when you reveal it to them they hear it clearly, accept it, and begin to take the right steps toward their new calling. In Jesus name we pray, Amen"

It is that easy. Once you become comfortable with prayer, you'll be untouchable. The enemy attacks our prayer life because he knows the power of prayer. He knows that if he can attach intimidation to prayer then he could potentially cut off communication between us and God. The enemy has had us bonded for years, influencing us to think that we weren't adequate enough to pray, or that our prayers weren't good enough. But today, I declare that that stronghold is BROKEN!

Now that you have prayed about your calling and purpose, you must have patience. Just because you asked God today does not mean you will find out tomorrow. Prayers have no expiration date; God will answer all of your prayers in His time. So, when you think it's too late to receive whatever it is that you have been praying for, I pray that you are reminded that God's timing is perfect. When you have been praying for so long and you have yet to see fruit, keep praying; don't let your impatience stop you from praying. Do not become doubtful. Do not allow your faith to waiver.

See, the key to prayer is believing in what you're praying for. You must pray like you're expecting your blessing to come. There is no room for doubtful prayers. Believe in every single prayer you send up. Mark 11:24 says "Therefore I tell you, whatever you ask for in prayer, believe that you have received it, and it will be yours."

If you're asking to be shown your purpose and calling,

believe that it will be revealed to you. If you've been praying to be delivered from sin, believe that you will be delivered and that the bonds will be broken.

A Thought and a Prayer

Do not be anxious for anything; but in everything by prayer and supplication with thanksgiving let your requests be made known to God.

Philippians 4:6

There is a distinct difference between the thoughts that float through our heads and prayers. Many of us do a lot of hoping. Hoping that our families will be tied back together, wishing our marriages will get better, hoping that our grades will get better, hoping to be healed, hoping to come across the right people that will invest in our business, hoping to get an internship. The difference between wishful thoughts and prayers is that thoughts include anxiety and prayer releases anxiety.

It is time that we turn those recurring thoughts and ideas into intentional prayers. The "God I pray you do a work in my life" prayers have served their season. It is time that we become purposeful with our prayers.

If you want and or need an investor to invest in your business pray for exactly that, "God I believe that you will send the right investor to interrupt me in my tracks. I thank you for closing every other door to those that you did not see fit to embark on this journey with me, and I thank you in advance for the person you are sending my way. I pray that when you send them you give me the wisdom to know they were sent specifically from you to me. In Jesus name I pray Amen!"

Do you see the difference between the two? Lift up the specific things that you need from God. No longer will we be conscious about our thoughts but we will be conscious about our prayers.

I know it's tough. The one and only thing you've been praying for and asking God for still hasn't come. However, stay strong, stay righteous, stay prayerful and remain committed to God. Just because you have not received what you've been praying for does not mean you can't have it, it just means it's not the time. So, don't give up, it's coming.

Waiting to Hear from God

And let us not be weary in well doing: for in due season we shall reap, if we faint not.
—*Galatians 6:9*

Why does God make us wait? God wants to teach us patience, elevate us and strengthen us in our faith. Though we may ask God to do these things, He works on His timing. So, what do we do when we're waiting to hear from God?

In the times in which we pray that God will bless our lives and our spirits, we are often subject to a waiting period. We plant our seeds, water them, tend to them daily, but we are so anxious to see them sprout that we stand over them so that we can watch them grow. We become distraught when they don't grow as fast as we would like them to and become discouraged and even doubtful that our seed is good. We even go as far as to start believing that our seeds will never grow.

In the time in which God is preparing our seeds to grow, or our blessings, we must stay focused on Him. We must continue in prayer, fasting, and work so that we do not become discouraged or distracted by the cares of the world. We must stay focused on the work that God has put in front of us, the work that God calls us to do at particular moments. With each task that God gives you, work diligently to ensure that that task is done to the best of your ability by handling it with the right amount of effort, care and attention. Don't be so focused on one seed that you do not realize that God is trying to give you other seeds that He needs you to plant.

So, in your time of waiting, simply continue working and have faith that all of your work and efforts will be blessed and called to completion.

The Cost of Your Calling

We must be willing to get rid of the life we've planned so we can have the life that is waiting for us.

Joseph Campbell

If no one told you, let me be the first to tell you—your calling has a cost. It may cost you friends, habits, your lifestyle, your job and even the life you planned for yourself.

In many situations, our own vision is the thing that blocks us from God moving in our lives. But in order to steer you toward your calling, God will interrupt your life. This is not to destroy you but to navigate you and lead you closer to where He wants you to be.

Your calling is going to cost you the life you think you want, but it's also going to give you exceedingly and abundantly above more than you could ever ask for in the life that you are destined to live. Your calling is going to cost you some relationships. God may decide that He wants you to detach from certain friends but the new people He's going to give you are so much better suit for where He's taking you. With elevation brings separation. So please don't be surprised when God begins to separate you from best friends, boyfriends, and girlfriends. The more you seek God, the more things you are exposed to. Your perspective begins to change, your position shifts, and your priorities are categorized differently.

Your calling comes at a cost, but you must be willing to sacrifice all that you have to receive all that God has for you. So, before you embark on this journey, count the cost and be prepared to leave your life behind, but note: everything that has to go, God is going to replace it with something so much better.

About the Author

Leah Hernandez is a junior Business Administration major at Clark Atlanta University. Born and raised in Southern California, Leah is CEO and Founder of Purposeful Millennials Publishing Company. She made this business to empower and develop a clientele of millennial bestselling authors. In a society that believes the millennial generation has gone through life aimlessly, she wants to promote and prove just how purposeful this generation can be. Leah lives her life by the words of Martin Luther King Jr.: "Love is the regulating factor." Leah's purpose is to love others and to allow God's light to shine through her. She plans to continuously outpour all the knowledge and wisdom that has been outpoured to her, to ensure that everyone is given the same and equal opportunities to excel.

Connect with Leah at trygodthebook.com.

About the Publisher

Purposeful Millennials Publishing

Purposeful Millennials Publishing Co. helps millennial authors publish their literary work. Our mission is to empower the millennial generation to walk in their purpose and publish their book. In an environment where everything we do is purposeful, we believe that we can be a guiding tool to shift this generation for the better. We are Christian-based and are guided by the word of God. To increase the number of best-selling millennial authors across the globe we empower millennials to use their purpose, writing, to help the lives of others.